Happy Birthday,
Dr. King!

by Kathryn Jones

Illustrated by
Floyd Cooper

SIMON & SCHUSTER BOOKS FOR YOUNG READERS
Published by Simon & Schuster
New York   London   Toronto   Sydney   Tokyo   Singapore

 SIMON & SCHUSTER BOOKS FOR YOUNG READERS
Simon & Schuster Building, Rockefeller Center, 1230 Avenue of the Americas, New York, New York 10020
Copyright © 1994 by The Children's Museum, Boston. Originally published by Modern Curriculum Press as
part of the Multicultural Celebrations series created under the auspices of The Children's Museum, Boston.
Leslie Swartz, Director of Teacher Services, organized and directed this project with funding from The
Hitachi Foundation. All rights reserved including the right of reproduction in whole or in part in any form.
Photographs: 5, Black Star / Flip Sarulke; 10, AP / Wide World Photos; 18, AP / Wide World Photos.
SIMON & SCHUSTER BOOKS FOR YOUNG READERS is a trademark of Simon & Schuster. Manufactured in Mexico.
Designed by Gary Fujiwara

10 9 8 7 6 5 4 3 2 1   ISBN: 0-671-87523-X

▲▲▲▲▲▲▲
The
〰〰〰
Children's
●●●●●
Museum
◆◆◆◆◆◆
Boston
〰〰〰

"Class, don't forget your assignment for tonight. Think about the Martin Luther King, Jr. assembly. His birthday is almost here," Mrs. Gordon said to her 4th grade class.

"Jamal, Arthur, you two wait. You have another assignment. Please take these notes from the principal home for your parents."

"A pink slip! I'm really in trouble now!" Jamal
thought to himself walking home through the January
slush. "Maybe Mom won't ask me about school."

Jamal decided to go in the front door and quietly upstairs
to his room. Usually, he liked that his mother was
home from her job at the hospital before he got home
from school. Today was different.

"Jamal, is that you? Is Alisha with you?" Mrs. Wilson called
from the kitchen.

"It's just me, Mom," Jamal answered.

"How did your day go?" she asked.

"Well, we're planning Dr. King's birthday celebration and I have some math and..." Jamal pulled the crumpled pink slip out of his pocket.

"A pink slip? Did you get into trouble?" she asked looking him straight in the eye. Grandpa Joe came into the kitchen.

"What's this I hear about trouble — and Dr. King?" he asked. "What's the pink paper?"

"It's just a note from the principal. It's no big deal." Jamal said.
"Yesterday I got into a fight with another kid on my bus. We
both wanted to sit in the back seat."

Grandpa Joe's smile disappeared.

"FIGHTING to sit at the BACK of the bus! I can't
believe what I'm hearing!" Grandpa Joe said in that voice
— that voice that tells the family to sit up and listen.

"Why would you want to fight over something like that?"
he said, walking toward the basement door. "I just can't
believe it."

"Why is Grandpa Joe so angry?" Jamal asked his mother.
"It's no big deal."

"It is a very big deal — especially to your grandfather.
Why don't you go and talk to him about it?"

6

"Grandpa Joe, I'm sorry that I got into trouble for fighting. I won't do it again."

"Jamal, you are ten years old and old enough to understand. It's almost Martin Luther King, Jr.'s birthday. What are you doing for the celebration this year?"

"What does Dr. King's assembly have to do with a little fight?"

Grandpa Joe took a deep breath and began...
"A long time ago I was raising my family in Montgomery, Alabama. This is what used to happen when African Americans wanted to ride the city buses.

"First, we'd get on at the front of the bus, pay our fare, and get off. Then we'd get back on again at the rear of the bus. We didn't like it, but that's how things were. It was the law. Then one day, in 1955, a lady named Rosa Parks..."

"Rosa Parks," Jamal interrupted, "we read about her. She sat in the front of the bus and wouldn't give her seat to a white man, and she got arrested."

"But, Jamal, there is more to the story. When African Americans heard about her arrest, many of us stopped riding the buses. We wanted to *protest* her arrest and get the same rights that white people had. That was the Montgomery Bus *Boycott*. And the boycott worked. We finally won — without fighting.

"Now, you go think about that bus boycott. Maybe you can figure out why I'm so unhappy about your pink slip."

"Jamal. Your sister's home. Come and set the table," Mrs. Wilson called. Jamal hurried up the stairs. He had some hard thinking to do.

10

"Heard you got into trouble," Alisha said to her brother.

"Oh, be quiet."

"Okay you two," said Jamal's Dad coming in. "Jamal knows he did something wrong. How is your homework going?"

"Well...we have to think of something to do for the Martin Luther King, Jr. assembly."

"Everyone in my class is learning parts of his 'I Have A Dream' speech," Alisha chimed in.

"I'll think of something. Grandpa Joe and I were talking about the bus boycotts."

"That should give you some ideas," his Dad said. "Did you know that Grandpa Joe took me to hear Dr. King speak when I was your age?"

"You heard Martin Luther King, Jr. yourself?" Jamal asked.

12

"I sure did. It was during the boycott, too. Grandpa Joe took me to a meeting at a church one night. This man went up to the front and suddenly everyone stood and clapped. Then, he started talking. I couldn't believe the power of his speech.

"That man was Dr. King. He told us why to boycott the buses, and how we needed to help each other. Dr. King became a great leader of the *civil rights* movement."

"I know about that part," Jamal said. "That's why we celebrate his birthday. But *how* to celebrate is the problem."

"Then remember, Dr. King always spoke out about peaceful ways to make things happen. Does that help?"

"Peaceful..." Jamal said slowly thinking. "You mean like not fighting? And those peaceful ideas worked back then?"

"Jamal, peaceful ideas work today, too," his Dad answered.

"Peaceful," Jamal said again and his face brightened. "That's it! Our class could do something to show that fighting is not the way to get things done. Maybe we could do a skit. Everyone could have a part and we could have costumes and I could be the star and..."

"Whoa," his Dad said. "First you'd better eat your dinner. Then you can write down your ideas for Mrs. Gordon."

"Grandpa Joe," Jamal asked as his grandfather joined them. "When you were a kid, did you ever do something *really* stupid that turned out to be *stupendous* instead?"

Grandpa Joe's smile returned and he nodded his head.

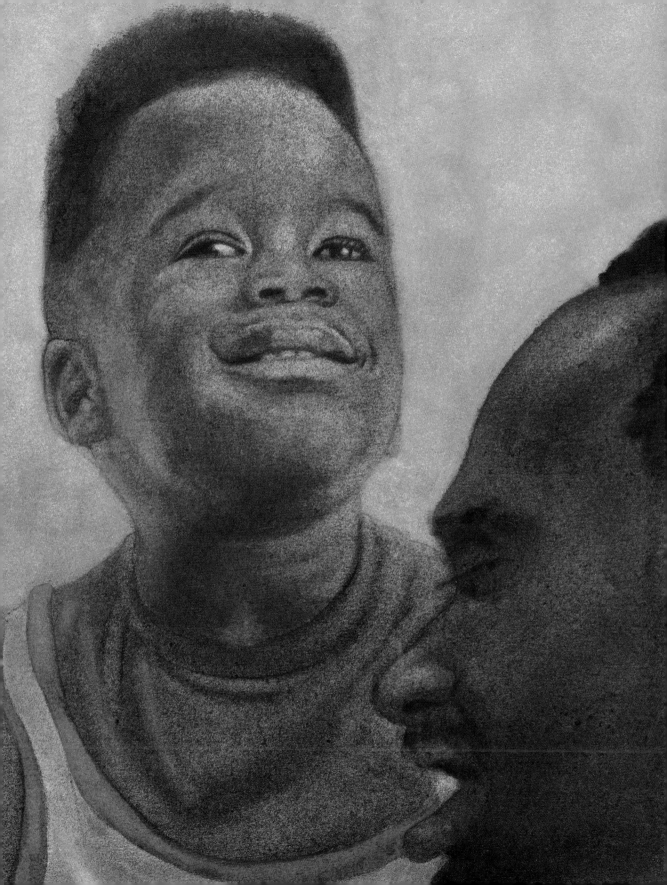

"All right children, settle down now. We have a lot of
work to do today," Mrs. Gordon said. "Let's start with the
Martin Luther King, Jr. birthday assembly. Who has an idea
for what our class can do? Oh — Jamal?"

Jamal stood proudly. "I have an idea for a skit. It's about
these two dopey boys who don't understand about Martin
Luther King, Jr. They get into a fight over a seat in the
back of the bus..."

Glossary

assembly (uh-SEHM-blee) a large group of people gathered together

boycott (BOY-kaht) people joining together and not buying or using something. They want to make a change happen by doing this.

civil rights (Si-vul-RITS) the legal rights of each citizen, such as the right to vote

protest (PRO-test) to speak out against something

stupendous (stoo-PEN-dahs) amazing, very great

About the Author

Kathryn Jones has explored her African American heritage since her early schooling at the Highland Park Free School and the Elma Lewis School of Fine Arts, both in Boston, Massachusetts. Currently working in The Children's Museum's Multicultural and Early Childhood Programs, Kathryn holds a degree in Elementary Education and English.

About the Illustrator

Floyd Cooper was born and raised in Tulsa, Oklahoma. He received a degree in fine arts from the University of Oklahoma and apprenticed under artist Mark English. After working for a greeting card company, Mr. Cooper moved to New York City to pursue a career as an illustrator of books for young people. His first book, *Grandpa's Face* (by Eloise Greenfield; Philomel, 1988) was named an American Association Notable Book for Children.